Julius Lester

Pharaoh's Daughter

A Novel of Ancient Egypt

SILVER WHISTLE
HARCOURT, INC.
San Diego   New York   London

Requests for permission to make copies of any part of the work should be mailed
to the following address: Permissions Department, Harcourt, Inc.,
6277 Sea Harbor Drive, Orlando, Florida 32887-6777.

Silver Whistle is a registered trademark of Harcourt, Inc.

Library of Congress Cataloging-in-Publication Data
Lester, Julius.
Pharaoh's daughter: a novel of ancient Egypt/by Julius Lester.
p.   cm.
"Silver Whistle."
Summary: A fictionalized account of a Biblical story in which
an Egyptian princess rescues a Hebrew infant who becomes a prophet of his people
while his sister finds her true self as a priestess to the Egyptian gods.
1. Egypt—Civilization—To 332 B.C.—Juvenile fiction.   2. Jews—History—
To 1200 B.C.—Juvenile fiction.   3. Moses (Biblical leader)—Juvenile fiction.
[1. Egypt—Civilization—To 332 B.C.—Fiction.   2. Jews—History—To 1200 B.C.—
Fiction.   3. Moses (Biblical leader)—Fiction.   4. Bible. O.T.—History of
Biblical events—Fiction.   5. Parent and child—Fiction.]   I. Title.
PZ7.L5629Ph   2000
[Fic]—dc21   99-6403
ISBN 0-15-201826-3

Designed by Linda Lockowitz
Text set in Weiss
First edition
A C E G H F D B
Printed in the United States of America

Pharaoh's Daughter

To
My Lady, Milan

Introduction

ONE QUESTION WRITERS are always asked is, "Where do you get your ideas?" I explain that fiction does not have its genesis in ideas but in feelings, and especially in a need to know something. I also explain that sometimes another person gives me an idea. So it was with this book.

Ms. Barbara Bader is a critic and librarian who reviewed a book of mine, *Sam and the Tigers,* for the *Horn Book,* the eminent journal of children's literature. Although we have never met, she called one afternoon to ask if I would undertake a picture-book retelling of the story of Moses, with Jerry Pinkney, who illustrated *Sam and the Tigers* and other books of mine.

Immediately I was reminded of Batya, the daughter of Pharaoh who finds the baby Moses in a basket in the river Nile and takes him to raise as her own son. In 1979, more than two years before I began studying for my eventual conversion to Judaism, I found myself spontaneously writing about this young woman for a lecture I was preparing for a class I taught then on Black-Jewish relations. Who was she? What motivated her to defy her father's orders that all Hebrew male babies were to be killed? I knew that the story I wanted to tell was too complex for a picture book, and thus this novel was born.

I wanted readers to experience Moses as a person. This is not easy because all of us have our associations with this figure, sometimes from religious school or films. It is difficult not to see Charlton Heston when one thinks of Moses. To free myself as writer from my own associations, I decided to spell Moses' name as Mosis, a shortened form of Tuthmosis. Mosis is a common suffix in ancient Egyptian, and often men were named for one of the many gods whose names carry that suffix. The suffix means "is born."

It seems that the writer of the Hebrew bible did not know that Mosis was the shortened form of an Egyptian name and associated it with the Hebrew verb *masha*, "to draw out." Thus, in the Hebrew bible, Pharaoh's daughter names the child Mosheh, "because I drew him out of the water." I have removed Moses from sacred history and have sought to put him into human history and thus thought it more accurate to spell his name as *Mosis* throughout this novel.

Writing this book became an experience that wholly involved me—intellectually, emotionally, spiritually. I became enthralled by ancient Egypt, a civilization that lasted some five thousand years and was probably as close to a paradise on earth as has ever been. But, more important, writing the novel became another journey into understanding who I was as I made the transition from my fifties and into my sixties. The courage to be who you are is something we learn and relearn throughout our decades, and perhaps that was why I had been drawn to the story of Pharaoh's daughter in 1979. Twenty years have passed and I am still learning who I am, still learning the courage to be.

Prologue

I SIT ON THE STONE BENCH in the garden of the Women's Palace. I have sat here almost every morning since I came to the palace fifteen years ago. Nothing has changed in all that time. The ibises wading in the lake could have been here when Ra'kha'ef built Hor-em-akhet a thousand years ago. In Khemet nothing changes. Past, present, and future merge and eternity is always now. At least that is how it was for me.

But I don't want to think about that. I want to sit here in peace, as I have every day after morning prayers. The baboons chatter quietly in the trees, their strenuous screeching to awaken Amon-Re, the sun god, finished for today. From inside the palace come faint sounds as the servants begin their morning chores. The white light of Amon-Re spreads farther and farther into the black sky. The god has survived another journey through the chaos of night.

Out of the corner of my eye, I notice someone come out of the palace. I turn to see who it is. I am surprised.

It is Batya, the oldest daughter of Pharaoh by his dead and still beloved wife, Queen Nefertari. Once Batya was called Meryetamun. For a while we were like sisters. Now we are not. However, there is respect. Sometimes that is better than love.

"Life, prosperity, and health!" I greet her in the usual way of Khemet.

"In peace, Almah," she returns weakly, not meeting my eyes.

Although we are no longer close, I know her well, and if Batya cannot look me in the eye, something is wrong. "What's the matter?"

"It's Mosis," she answers.

"Mosis? Has something happened to him?" I ask, getting to my feet, wanting to go to him.

Batya holds up a hand as if to restrain me. "He is not hurt. It is something else."

"Well, what?" I demand to know. "Tell me what is going on!" I am almost beside myself with worry and frustration. Why is she being so evasive?

"I would rather we were inside. Let me go to my suite. Wait a little and then join me there. It would be better if no one saw us going in together."

"Very well," I agree reluctantly, sitting down again. Why is she playing this game? Intrigue is not a part of Batya's nature. Something serious has happened. But what? Why doesn't she want anyone to see us together? Or is it that she wants to be certain that the just-returned Queen Asetnefret does not see us together? That must be it. Because I have not lived in the Women's Palace for many years, my being seen there would attract attention, and there is seldom a reward for being noticed by Asetnefret.

ENOUGH TIME HAS PASSED. And even if it hasn't, I can't wait any longer. I get up and, making sure no one is around, go casually but quickly into the palace and to the suite on the second floor where I lived with Batya when I first came here. No one has seen me. Without knocking I let myself in.

My brother sits on a couch, his head down. Batya is beside him. Although I see him every day, I still can't believe how much like a Khemetian he looks. The short wig fits his head as if he had been born into it. Even sitting, his height is apparent as well as his muscled torso and strong legs beneath the linen kilt. With the gray makeup around his eyes, he would look Khemetian to anyone who did not know, look as if he had been born into the house of Pharaoh.

Unfortunately this picture of Khemetian perfection is broken when Mosis speaks. There is no physical defect in his mouth and there are times when he gets so excited or angry that words pour out of his mouth like water from a fountain. But usually he speaks as if his tongue were as heavy as a stone in a pyramid.

"Mosis?" I say softly. "What is it?"

There is a long pause. He does not act as if he has heard me, though I know he has. Finally he says, "I murdered."

3

His head is down and the words are mumbled. I am not sure I heard what he said. "You did what?"

"I murdered."

His voice has the dull hollowness of footsteps in a tomb. I was not mistaken. That is what I heard the first time. I do not understand. I look from him to Batya, who holds his hands in hers. Mosis? My brother? Killed someone? "That—that doesn't make any sense," I say, bewildered, looking from one to the other. "What are you talking about?"

Mosis looks at Batya. She says, "I don't know. He will not tell me."

I still do not understand. Murder? In Khemet? That is unheard of. I go over and stoop down beside him. "Mosis," I say, taking his hands out of Batya's and holding them in mine. "What happened? What's going on? Please. Talk to me."

"Last night," Mosis answers.

"'Last night'? Yes. Go on."

He starts to cry.

"Kakemour," he whispers in a voice as dry as sand.

"What did you say?" I ask, feeling suddenly lightheaded.

"Kakemour," he repeats.

"You killed Kakemour?" I ask, panic rising in me at what this will mean.

He nods reluctantly.

"Why, Mosis?" I ask. "Why? What happened?"

Part One

Part One

Chapter One

MY PARENTS TALKED in the darkness for a long time, their voices moving in and out of my sleep like the back of a hippopotamus rising and sinking in the Great Hapi. Abba, Father, spoke softly and slowly, while Ima, Mother, talked rapidly, as if she had to get all the words out before she forgot them. My brother Aharon, and sister, Miryam, are seven and four and hear nothing, not even the sounds of their own sleep. My baby brother, Yekutiel, is barely three months old. He sleeps through everything.

I am Almah, and I used to sleep like Yekutiel, but now that I am twelve I lie awake in the darkness. Something is wrong. Every evening after Abba comes home from working on the pharaoh's temple in Pi-Ramesses, men come to talk. My father is named Amram, and he is a leader of our people, the Habiru, "the people from the other side." ("The other side of what?" I asked him once. He said we have a land of our own, and one day our god, Ya, will send a redeemer who will lead us out of Khemet and into our land. Abba said that in our land the rivers

flow with milk and honey. When I asked, "What is a redeemer and when is he coming?" he looked away.) Abba
and the men talk long into the darkness, but their voices
are low and I cannot hear their words. Yesterday I asked
Ima what they were talking about. She looked at me as if
I were bad luck that had come to life.

I get up when I see the blackness on the ceiling
change to gray. Miryam has a leg on top of mine, an
arm flung across my chest. Aharon lies pressed against
me on the other side. Abba snores softly. Gently I move
Miryam's arm and leg and get up. She and Aharon do not
waken, but they sense I am leaving and move closer to
each other. Aharon has only a little while longer to sleep
before it will be time for him to get up and go with Abba
to work in Pi-Ramesses.

Rubbing my eyes I walk into the kitchen and get the
water jar. I go out the back door, past the bread oven
built against the house, through the doorway in the wall,
and into the narrow street. Pale pink tinges the eastern
sky where the sun will rise.

Our house is on the corner of the Street of the Ser-
pent and the Street of the River, at the farthest end of the
village. It faces the Great Hapi, though at a safe distance.
The river has started rising, which means the new year
has begun. In Khemetian it is called the season of Akhet.
The river will rise until it threatens to flow over the top
of the road that protects us. That has never happened,
though. But for almost two months it will be as if we
are living next to the Great Green Sea. Then slowly, so
slowly that we will not notice at first, the river will return

to its bed and leave behind the thick black mud in which we will plant.

Other girls and women walk by me, water jars atop their heads like hair piled high, on their first of many trips to the river for water. Though one or two glance at me, they do not speak.

Instead of following them, I cross the street to a small path and disappear among the canebrake and the long sharp leaves of the papyri that tower above me. The birds send warning calls from the tops of the papyri. I would think they would know me by now.

Eventually I come to a stream, one of the branches of the Great Hapi where the river is not as wide or deep. The others are afraid to come here for water. Because of the snakes. They say I come here because I think I am better than anybody else and don't want to be around them. (*"Who cares if you can speak Khemetian? If you were a real Habiru, you would not speak the language of people who hate us."*) I tried to explain that it is quiet here and that I like the music of the silence and the music of the birds. They did not believe me. Perhaps because I was not telling the truth.

I look carefully for any snakes or crocodiles that might be hiding in the thick bulrushes. Then, looking around once more to be sure no one is watching, I take off my dress and face the sun. It seems to be reaching for me through the papyri as its warmth pours over my new-swelling breasts and the wispy hair that says I am becoming a woman.

This is the real reason I come here for water. I have never told anyone. It is my secret. Mine and the sun's. I raise my arms high over my head and move them outward in a circle as if I am holding the sun, but it does not burn me because I love it and it loves me. I close my eyes and tongues of warmth cover my body. I think I could stand here like this for the rest of my life.

However, sooner than I would like, I get nervous that someone will see me. I know they can't, but that does not matter. I force my eyes open and slip my dress on. Then I fill the jar, put it on my head, and start for home.

When I reach the kitchen, I pour the water into a larger jug. I will carry water from the river many times today until the big jug is filled. Now, however, I take the bread, cucumbers, and dried fish from the baskets where they are kept, slice them, and put them on a reed plate. Then, filling a bowl with water, I go up the stairs to the roof, where Abba is kneeling and facing the sun.

Each morning, when he hears me go out to get water Abba gets up. He likes to begin the day praising and thanking Ya. It looks as if he is praying to the sun, but the Habiru are not like Khemetians, who say the sun is a god named Amon-Re. Abba says the sun is a light in the sky that Ya made.

I put Abba's breakfast down. His eyes are closed and his lips move rapidly, but I cannot hear any words. I squat nearby and wait.

Before long Abba opens his eyes, turns, and smiles at me. "Good morning, Almah."

"Good morning, Abba."

I hand him his breakfast. He sits down opposite me

and crosses his legs, his back to the sun. "We must talk, Almah," he begins, tearing off a piece of bread and putting it in his mouth.

His voice is quiet and serious. I am scared, wondering what I did wrong.

"How old are you now?"

"Twelve." Why is he asking me something he knows the answer to?

He nods. "You are almost a woman." He bites into a slice of cucumber.

Now I know what this is about—he has chosen a husband for me. I don't care who it is. I won't marry him or anybody, not now. Not ever!

"Ima and I need your help." His face is almost mournful.

What is the matter? Is he sick? Ima? What is wrong? "What do you want me to do, Abba?" I ask, afraid to hear the answer.

He smiles, but his smile is weak, like the moon on the nights when it is shrinking. He drinks deeply from the bowl of water. With his long hair and big dark beard, I imagine that Ya looks like Abba. (Ima said, "Ya does not look like anything, and certainly not like a man.") He is big and his muscles are as hard as sun-dried bricks because he helps move the heavy stones for the temple. But his eyes are soft and kind. Not like Ima's.

"I'm sure you have been wondering why all the men have been coming to our house in the evenings and what Ima and I talk about late into the night."

Of course! All those men have sons, and Abba and Ima have been whispering in the night trying to decide which one I should marry. I would rather die!

"This is not easy to talk about," Abba continues. "I find it hard to believe myself." He is speaking Khemetian now. He does this when he wants to make me feel that I am special to him. Since before I can remember, Abba has spoken to me in Khemetian, which he learned when he started working in Pi-Ramesses as a boy. When I used to go to the market there with Ima, I interpreted for her and many of the other Habiru women. But they still don't like me. ("Khemetian is the language of people who hate Ya," Ima says. Abba says it is the language of the people we live among: "We should know what they are saying and be able to talk to them." Ima is afraid that if I speak Khemetian I will become one. That is what she says. I think she doesn't like that Abba and I can talk and she doesn't know what we're saying.)

"There is a rumor that Pharaoh is going to have all newborn Habiru baby boys killed."

I do not understand. Is that what all the whispering and talking has been about? I am relieved but a little disappointed, too. I am old enough to marry. Even if I don't want to, why hasn't someone come and asked Abba for me? "That doesn't make sense," I say aloud. "Why would the pharaoh want to kill all the baby boys?"

Abba shakes his head. "Perhaps because we do not worship him as the other foreigners in Khemet do. Ya says we must worship only him and none other. Maybe that is why Pharaoh dislikes us. I do not know, Almah.

12

Who am I to understand the mind of Ramesses? But the *why* does not matter. If the rumor is true, we must make sure his soldiers do not find your little brother, or anyone else's. This is why Ima and I are going to need you more than ever."

"What do you want me to do?" I ask seriously.

"To watch out for the soldiers so they don't surprise us."

I want to help, but since Yekutiel was born, I have been doing a lot of the work Ima always did. "How can I do that and also get water, grind the grain and make bread, weave baskets, dishes, and cloth?" I complain.

"I know. This is more important. Your mother will manage," he reassures me. "We need you to keep a lookout. You won't be alone. All the girls who are not married will also be watching."

"What do I do if I see any soldiers?"

"Run to as many houses as you can and warn people so they can hide the babies."

"But where will they hide them?"

"In baskets, which they will put among the canes and bulrushes and cattails along the banks of the river."

"When do I start?"

"Today. We do not know when the soldiers are coming. Or if they are coming. But we must be ready."

AT FIRST IT IS EXCITING. Children run this way and that through the streets, looking for soldiers. But by the time the sun reaches the top of the sky, the smaller ones are tired and bored and are playing more than they are looking. By the next day, and certainly the one after, even many of the girls my age are doing more talking and giggling than looking.

A few days later, just as I think Abba is mistaken about the soldiers, I am standing in the road and there in the distance, where the broad paved road of Pi-Ramesses changes to the narrow dirt one of Goshen, I see figures. The only time so many people would be coming to Goshen is when the men come back from working in Pi-Ramesses, and it is too early for that. I run down the road until I can see them clearly. Soldiers! They walk two by two, the sunlight flashing off their upright spears like a warning. Wearing only loincloths, their bodies look so powerful, as if they will kill us with the mere appearance of their muscles.

I run back up the road as fast as I can and am almost out of breath when I burst into the house. "Ima! Ima! Soldiers! We must hurry!"

Ima comes out of the middle room, where we sleep. Sucking her thumb, Miryam is clutching Ima's skirt. Ima puts her finger to her lips, asking me to be quiet so as not to wake Yekutiel, as if anything could. "Where are they?"

"Just crossing into Goshen."

"Go back and keep watch. They may not come this far today."

I hurry back. I do not see any soldiers now. Where did they go? All I see is a lone figure in the distance. I don't hear any sounds from the village, either, but I do see an occasional figure run across the road and down the embankment to the river, carrying a basket and then returning with empty arms.

I continue looking for the soldiers. Only when I am almost out of Goshen do I see them at the far end of the Street of Avraham, going in and out of houses. They do not seem to be in a hurry. I hide on the riverbank just below the road to watch. Glancing up and down the river, I can see baskets among the thick stalks of the bulrushes and papyrus plants. But I see them only because I know what to look for. The soldiers will not see anything except bulrushes and papyri.

I see two soldiers on a rooftop. One holds a struggling woman while the other shoves his spear through a closed basket. The woman screams so loud I am surprised the river does not rise up to see what is wrong.

I . . . I do not want to see any more. I get up to go and, a short distance away, see a woman staring into the river. It must be the figure I saw earlier.

I have never seen anyone so beautiful. Her hair is plaited in many long tight braids that look like strands of night as they stream onto her shoulders and down her back. From beneath her hair large golden earrings flash like sunlight on the water. Around her head is a band of blue and red stones, and she has on a necklace like her headband; but these stones are larger, each one surrounded by a strip of gold, and it lies against her chest like the curve of the sun. Her eyes are large and the upper eyelids are painted dark gray, while the lower lids are painted dark green. The two colors meet at the corners of her eyes and extend outward in a line that goes almost as far back as her hair. Her lips are painted red, as if she took the color from the setting sun. I wonder if she is a goddess.

What is she doing here? Is she lost? I wonder if I should ask her, but it is none of my business. Then, just as I am about to turn away, I see her body tense. She is looking at something in the water. Suddenly she puts the back of her hand against her lips and opens her mouth, but no sound comes out. Instead she slumps to the ground as if a ray of sun has pierced her heart into stillness.

Without thinking I run up the embankment and onto the road. When I reach her I look down into the water. It is red. Green and white pieces of a basket float on the water, and I see the round bulging eyes of a crocodile as it disappears into the dark, bloody coldness.

Chapter Two

I WANT TO GO BACK TO BED and give this day a chance to start over again and be better. But the Khemetian woman's eyes flutter open slowly and get big when she sees me.

"It's—it's all right," I say in Khemetian.

She frowns. "You are Habiru?"

"Yes."

She shakes her head slowly, as if this is a bad dream from which she must awake. Where else would a Habiru girl be speaking Khemetian? With effort she sits up. "I . . . I must go. I should not be here. I am Princess Meryetamun. I am Pharaoh's daughter."

Now *my* eyes grow large. I was right. She *is* a goddess. If the pharaoh is a god, would not his daughter be a goddess? But the pharaoh is not a god. Ya is. But what if the pharaoh really is a god? Should I bow? No. Ya might kill me. Or Ima.

"Which way is Pi-Ramesses?"

That is when I know she is not well. Pi-Ramesses is in

the direction she is looking. "Would the princess like to come to my house and rest for a while?"

"No!" she exclaims. "I asked you a question. Which direction is Pi-Ramesses?"

I point. She looks. Then she turns in the other direction. "I am confused," she admits; her voice is small and weak now. She starts to stand up. I offer my hand but she ignores it. The princess is almost to her feet when her knees give way and she slumps to the ground again.

I do not know what to do. I want to get help but am afraid to leave her. Crocodiles move on land as easily and as quickly as they swim in the river. Sometimes they walk along this road as if going to work in Pi-Ramesses.

"A little water, perhaps," I suggest.

"Yes. Yes. That would be good," she admits. Her face is as white as the moon's on a night when it shines like the sun.

She gets up slowly. I offer my hand again.

"No one is allowed to touch the pharaoh or a member of his family," she says. "The penalty for doing so is death."

I am not sure I heard her correctly. "I am sorry, Princess. Could you repeat what you said . . . slowly?"

She does so, and I say again to myself in Habiru to make sure I understand. I do. So, whenever she stumbles and almost loses her balance, I do not try to catch her. Eventually we reach our house.

"Ima! Ima!" I call excitedly as the princess walks unsteadily inside and slumps to the floor.

Ima comes hurrying from the other room, Yekutiel in

her arms, Miryam hiding behind her legs. Ima is startled to see the Khemetian woman and shoves Yekutiel into Miryam's arms, then pushes her out of sight. Quickly I tell Ima everything that happened and who the woman is.

"You fool!" Ima snaps when I am finished. "You were supposed to warn me when the soldiers were coming. Instead you bring Pharaoh's own daughter into our house! What were you thinking?"

I . . . I do not know what to say. Ima is right; I did not think. But looking at the princess sitting on the reed-matted floor, like a little girl who needs her mother, I do not know what else I was supposed to have done.

"Well, now that she is here, perhaps a little kindness from us will lead her to seek kindness for us from her father, the butcher of children! Get her some water."

I run to the kitchen and return quickly with a pitcher and bowl. I fill the bowl and hand it to the princess. She does not notice.

"Princess?" I say softly.

She blinks her eyes, and it is as if she wakes up and sees where she is for the first time. I notice that Ima has gone into the middle room. "What is your name?" the princess asks.

"Almah."

"Thank you, Almah," she says, taking the bowl from me and drinking. When she is finished I refill the bowl. She empties it. I fill it again and this time she drinks more slowly. Finally she puts the bowl on the floor and looks around.

I am ashamed as I look at my home and myself

through her eyes. It is a dark and narrow room, with only a little light coming in through the small oblong windows near the ceiling. The mud-brick walls are bare, and the only furniture is the low table on which we put the food when we eat. The reed mats covering the floor are worn. If I did not have to be out looking for soldiers, I would be gathering reeds to make new ones. And what must I look like to her—a thin female, no longer a child, not yet a woman, with black curly hair and eyes as dark as mud. Sometimes I look at my face when getting water from the river, and my lips are too full and my nose too narrow for me to be pretty. But if I were ugly, at least one girl in the village would have been glad to tell me by now. Perhaps it is worse than I think, since no one has ever told me that I am pretty or ugly. No one except Abba, who says I am beautiful.

"How are you feeling?" I ask, not wanting her to think anymore about how this room or I look.

"Better," she says.

It is true. Her face is not so pale.

Just then the door opens. It is Abba and Aharon. When my brother sees the princess, his eyes get large, like hers when she saw me. Aharon looks up at Abba, then runs from the room.

Abba's eyes narrow as he looks from the princess to me. Before he can wonder if Yekutiel is safe, I tell him in Habiru what happened and the tension leaves his face.

Abba turns to the princess. "I am Amram," he introduces himself in Khemetian.

"I am Meryetamun, the daughter of Pharaoh."

"My daughter explained to me that you were not feeling well and needed to rest. Welcome to our home."

"Thank you. Your Khemetian is nearly perfect."

"You flatter me. I learned your language some years ago, as a boy, when I began working in Pi-Ramesses. May we offer you something to eat? Some fruit? Grapes? Apples?"

"Grapes would be delicious. Perhaps I am more hungry than anything else."

I hurry back to the kitchen and return with a basket of grapes.

The princess eats slowly. "Almah?" she asks after a while.

"Yes, Princess?"

"When you found me this afternoon, did . . . did you see anything?"

I know what she is asking. What should I say? I want to look at Abba. He would know how to answer. But the princess is looking directly at me. " 'See anything'?" I repeat.

"In the water. Did you see anything?"

"Such as?"

"A basket, perhaps?"

I feel Abba looking at me and I know I must not tell her the truth. She wants to know how we are hiding the babies so she can tell the soldiers what to look for. "Did the princess lose something in the river?"

"Never mind," she says abruptly. I cannot tell if she thinks I am stupid or lying.

Suddenly, from the other room Yekutiel lets out a squeal that is quickly muffled.

21

"Was that a baby? Didn't I see a baby when I came in?" the princess asks.

"I heard nothing," Abba says.

The princess gets to her feet. Now she looks like one who could tell the sun to stop shining and it would obey. "Almah. Your mother was standing there, holding a baby, when I first came in."

"The sun will be down soon, Princess," Abba says quietly but firmly. "Everyone at the palace must be concerned about the daughter of Pharaoh. Isn't it unusual for the Royal Daughter to be in Goshen among the Habiru? And without servants? I would not want your father, Lord of the Two Lands and the Bringer of Light, to think unkind thoughts because his daughter ventured unbidden into our village. Almah will walk back with you so you will not lose your way."

Abba's voice is smooth, like lotion, and I can see the princess becoming soft beneath his words.

"You speak well, Amram," she says, smiling slightly. "I...I did not mean any harm to your wife—or your baby. I only wanted to see the child."

"If there were a child to see, Princess, it would have been our honor to show her to you."

I start to say the baby is a him but realize in time that Abba does not want the princess to know the truth.

It is late afternoon as the princess and I leave. Many people walk along the road as the workers return from Pi-Ramesses. Everyone stares at us. Some recognize me, and I hear them whispering, "Isn't that the daughter of Amram? Of course she would be with a Khemetian!"

Walking next to the princess with everyone looking at us, I feel something I have never felt in my life. I feel important.

"How old are you, Almah?" the princess asks me.

"Twelve."

"You seem older. I would have thought you were at least my age, but I can see now that your breasts are only beginning."

"May I ask how old you are, Princess?"

"Fifteen."

She is a woman. "You are married?" I ask her.

She looks down at me. "Why do you ask?"

I don't know what to say. Most girls are married by the time they are twelve. But maybe it is different if you are a princess. "I wanted to know what it is like to be married," I say finally.

"I don't know. There is someone who would marry me, but I don't think I want to marry him—or anyone."

"Me, too!" I exclaim excitedly. "Me, too!"

She laughs. I do not know what is so funny, but I am pleased that I made her laugh.

"And why would you not want to marry?" she asks me.

"I just don't."

She laughs again, but this time it is quieter. "That's probably the best reason there is. But don't you want to have children?"

I start to tell her how much I took care of Aharon when he was little, and Miryam and Yekutiel now, but I stop myself. "I'm not sure."

"If you do not have children, what will happen to you?"

I do not understand. "What do you mean?"

"What do the Habiru do to women who do not have children?"

I still do not understand. "Nothing. I mean, I don't know. Why would someone do something to you because you didn't have a child?"

"Among my people, having children is so important that some men kill themselves if they do not become fathers. A woman who does not have a child is called Mother of the Absent One."

I do not want to be anyone's mother, present or absent.

Ahead of us I see the entrance to Pi-Ramesses. The inscribed pylons rise high into the sky to form a gateway. On each side are two huge statues of the pharaoh sitting in a chair as if he is judging every person who passes. This is the Avenue of the Pharaoh, and as we pass beneath the pylon, the road widens and is now made of large stones. On both sides huge statues hover as far as I can see. Some are lions with the faces of men. Others are men with the heads of rams, or birds and women balancing the sun on their heads between two curved horns. Mostly, though, there are huge statues of the pharaoh, these of him standing, his left leg forward. I should go back now, but it has been so long since I was last here.

Before Yekutiel was born, I would come to the market with Ima to swap vegetables and baskets for grain, fruit, and flax. Women still come to the house and ask Ima if I can go to market with them. They get more when I do the bargaining because I speak Khemetian, but Ima won't let me go with them. She is afraid of what I might learn or do if I go to Pi-Ramesses without her.

She is right. Whenever my bare feet touched the stones of Pi-Ramesses, I felt safer than when I walked in the dust and dirt of Goshen. I also liked looking at the statues of Khemetian gods. I wanted to know their names, what they did, and why the statues were so huge. Ima didn't want me to look at them. (*"How can people be so foolish as to worship a man with the head of a bird?"*) I thought it was easier to believe in a god that looked kind of like something you knew than one you couldn't see.

I would love to come into the city and go anywhere I wanted. I don't even know how big Pi-Ramesses is. Abba said it is divided into four sections, each one dedicated to a different god or goddess. Each has its own temple where the priests do rituals. In the center is the main temple, the one Abba and Aharon are helping build. The marketplace is outside that temple. I have never seen anything like it. It has columns so tall I cannot see their tops. And the columns are so big around that if two men with long arms stood on each side and put their arms around one, their fingertips would not meet. From here I can just see the golden dome of the main temple shining like the sun when it is at the top of the sky.

In every direction there are buildings, mostly houses. Grain is stored in the larger ones, Abba told me. During the day the street is crowded with people and animals carrying goods from the boats docked at the wharf, which I see in the distance to my right. Now, however, it is late and there are not many people about.

We come to another street. I really should turn back. But what if the princess starts to feel faint again? And if the princess didn't want me to come this far, she would have said something. So, she must want me to stay with her until she is home safely. I follow the princess along a street that is even broader than the Avenue of the Pharaoh. The stones here are very smooth, almost like glass. They are painted red, white, and green. On either side are date and palm and sycamore trees, grass as smooth as the river at the Season of the Inundation, and statues of the pharaoh leading to a long white wall stretching farther than I can see. The sun shines brightly off the gold-domed roof of a building behind the walls.

"That is the pharaoh's palace," the princess tells me, pointing at the golden dome.

I follow her until we stop before two large doors on which are painted a lotus and a papyrus plant in white, blue, and green.

"Come in," says the princess. "The sun will be going down soon. You could stay here in the palace tonight and return home in the morning. I could show you around the Women's Palace and the main palace where the pharaoh lives."

"The women have their own separate palace?" I ask, amazed.

The princess smiles. "Come. Let me show you."

I want so much to say yes, but I shake my head. "Ima and Abba would worry." Then I remember: She is Pharaoh's daughter. Her father wants to kill my brother. But she seems so nice. I start to walk away, but I start crying. I want to stay in the palace with her because I like her and wish I could be like her and Ima will be angry at me for bringing her to our house and I wish I didn't like her and I wish the sun wasn't as red as a baby's blood.

I stop. When I turn around she is staring after me and I want to run to her. Instead I yell, "There were pieces of straw scattered all over the water! And there was blood, lots and lots and lots of blood!" And I run away as fast as I can, tears streaming down my face.

Chapter Three

WHEN I GET HOME the front room is filled with men sitting on the floor who start shouting at me as soon as I walk in.

"What did she say?"

"Tell us. Tell us. Is she going to send the army?"

I do not understand what they are talking about or why they are shouting at me as if I have done something wrong. I am too old to cry and I am afraid I might, but just then I feel a hand on my shoulder. Abba! I wish he would pick me up and hold me like he does Miryam, like he used to hold me. Instead he raises his arms and everyone quiets.

"So, my daughter," he begins, smiling at me. "It is not every day that one of us talks with the daughter of Pharaoh. Everyone is eager to know what she said."

"About what?" I ask.

Abba chuckles. "About anything."

I would tell Abba everything but I don't want these other men to know. It was private, a conversation between two women. "We didn't talk much."

"Did she ask you any questions? Questions about us?" someone asks anxiously.

I shake my head. "No."

"No?" many voices respond, as if they don't believe me.

"Quiet!" Abba orders. "Go on, Almah."

"We didn't talk much. She wanted me to spend the night at the palace and said she would show me everything, but I told her that you and Ima would worry about me." I stop abruptly.

"Go on! Go on!" come the cries.

I look up at Abba, hoping he will tell me that I don't have to tell them more, but he says, "Is there something else, Almah? It is important that we know."

"I told her about the crocodile that killed the baby this afternoon," I continue, looking only at him, "and about all the blood that was on the water and how I didn't know a little baby was filled with so much blood, Abba."

There are gasps of shock and surprise. When it is quiet again, Abba asks, "And what did the princess say?"

"I . . . I . . . I don't know, Abba. I was angry and I was afraid and I ran." My voice is small. I bury my face against him and he puts an arm around me.

"This is outrageous!" someone exclaims. "Because of an impudent brat, we're all going to be killed!"

There is much shouting and talking, and I want to cover my ears. Why are they angry at me? I didn't do anything!

Abba raises his arms again and everyone is quiet. "Now, gentlemen," he says in a loud voice, "let us not get carried away by fear. The princess could have asked my daughter any question she wanted about where we were hiding the children, and she did not. What more proof do you want that she did not come here to spy on us?"

The shouting and yelling begin again. I am very tired and sleepy, and I slip into the middle room to look for Ima, but she isn't there. I find her and the children on the roof. She is sitting facing the doorway I've just come through. Aharon, Miryam, and Yekutiel are asleep beside her.

"Ima?" I say softly. As I get closer I can see that she is looking at me as if I do not belong to her.

I go to lie down between Aharon and Miryam as always.

"Are you trying to wake them up?" Ima hisses. She moves her arm angrily, as if shooing away a mosquito. I don't know what to do. Her arm sweeps out again as if knocking flies off carrots. I go to the far edge of the roof and lie down. What did I do to her? If I had known she would be angry at me even though I didn't stay at the Women's Palace, I would have stayed.

I don't remember falling asleep, but I am awakened by loud shouting from inside the house. It is Abba and Ima! I . . . I can't believe it. I have never heard them yell at each other. Then I hear my name. They are fighting about me! Ima is doing most of the shouting. I put my hands over my ears and close my eyes tightly. The next thing I know, my eyes open just as the sky is changing from black to gray.

I sit up and look around. I am alone on the roof. Then I remember Abba and Ima shouting at each other about me and I feel sick in my stomach. I don't want to get up. I don't want to go inside. But already I hear doors opening and closing from other houses and the soft fall of feet on the dirt street.

I go down the stairs quietly. I do not want them to hear me. I do not want them to know I am alive. But I hear them talking softly. Have they been awake all night talking about me?

"I am afraid." Ima's voice trembles as if she is about to cry.

"She is a good daughter. Almah works as hard as any girl in the village. Harder! Whatever you ask her to do, she does. And she never complains."

"I know. I know. But she frightens me."

"What do you mean?"

"Yesterday. Did you see?"

"See what?"

"She was not afraid, Amram. She was not afraid of the princess."

"And that frightens you? I don't understand."

"Don't you see? Any other girl in this village would have left a wealthy-looking Khemetian woman lying in the road, and run home and told her mother. No Habiru girl would have brought a Khemetian into her home without permission. But it did not occur to Almah that she had done something wrong. Even now she doesn't think she made a mistake. That is what frightens me."

"But isn't that what Ya wants us to do? Haven't we taught her to care about others? Haven't we taught her that she should be afraid of no one except Ya?"

31

"Yes. Yes."

"Then, what?"

There is a long silence. Finally I hear Ima say, "Maybe if you had not taught her Khemetian . . . But she is more your daughter than mine, anyway," she says, her voice aching with hurt.

Abba laughs uncomfortably. "That is not true, Yocheved." *But it is, Abba,* I say silently. "I did not set out to teach her Khemetian. It just happened. She took to the language so readily. And I've been thinking, what Almah did yesterday might save us."

Abba's voice drops to a whisper and I can no longer hear. Quietly, I go back up the stairs to the roof. There is a broad arc of white on the horizon at the place where the sun will rise. In the distance baboons are shrieking. The Khemetians believe the cries of the baboons awaken Amon-Re, the sun god. I wish they would let him sleep this morning. I don't want another day like yesterday. I thought I was doing the right thing. There wasn't time to be afraid or run home and ask Ima what I should do.

Then I realize: Ima cannot know what I should have done. She was not there. She did not see the crocodile's round eyes, the bits of basket floating on the bloody water. She did not see the princess fall to the earth as if she were dead. I did. Just because she is my mother, it does not mean she is always right.

I hear footsteps. It is Abba.

"Good morning." He smiles.

I do not smile back. "I'm sorry I overslept. I will get your breakfast and then go for water."

As I start to move past him, he puts out an arm and stops me. "What's the matter, Almah?"

His voice is soft and he looks worried. My bottom lip starts to tremble. I am going to cry and I don't want to. "Ima wasn't there, Abba. She can't know what I should have done." I say it in Khemetian so, if she is listening, she won't understand. The tears roll down my face, but I choke back any sound because I am afraid that what will come out will not be sobs but screams. I am so angry and so sad.

Abba pulls me to him and hugs me tightly to his chest, and now the sounds come but they are soft cries. "Why does Ima hate me, Abba?" I ask in a voice as tiny as a grain of sand.

"Oh, Almah! Your mother doesn't hate you. Don't ever think that! I know she is harsh with you sometimes. But that is because she loves you so much."

"No she doesn't, Abba," I answer, unafraid of what I am saying.

Abba takes my hand and we walk to the edge of the roof overlooking the street and sit, our backs against the wall. "Your mother does not see yet that you are almost a woman, that we will be finding a husband for you soon. She misses her little girl."

"That's not it, Abba. She doesn't like me because I know things she doesn't. She doesn't like me because I'm not like her. I'm different."

Abba blushes and tries to laugh. That's what adults do when they don't know what to say. "That is not so," he answers, but nothing in his voice makes me believe him.

"We will talk about this more at another time. Right now there is something else I need to talk with you about."

I wipe my eyes and look up at him.

"I need to know what else you and the princess talked about on your walk back to the palace. You were not telling everything."

"It was—well, you know—just something that girls talk about."

Abba smiles. "Oh, really? Like sisters?"

"Yes! *That's it!*" I exclaim, understanding now why I feel close to her. "She wanted to know how old I am. She's fifteen, but she's not married and she said she doesn't want to get married and I told her I didn't either. And then she wanted to know what will happen to me if I don't get married and have children. I didn't understand, but she said that Khemetians have to have children or they are called bad names. Abba, did you know that the princess lives in a separate palace called the Women's Palace?"

"No, I didn't. Would you like to live in a place that was just for women?"

"Maybe," I answer.

"Well, the next time you see the princess, if she asks to show you the Women's Palace, it would be all right with me if you went."

"Really?"

"Really."

My excitement dwindles quickly, though, as I remember the last thing I said to her. "I'll never see the princess again. Not after what I said to her."

34

"Don't be sure. I have a feeling the princess is going to come looking for you. If you need a big sister, she might need a little one. You and I like the princess and trust her. Everyone else thinks she came to spy on us. Your mother thinks she may have been pretending to be ill to get inside one of our homes. Ima even wonders if the pharaoh knows I am a leader of our people and sent her to find where we live."

"What do you think, Abba?"

"I believe Ya sent her and he also sent you to her."

"He *did*?"

He nods. "I think he did. Usually it is Ima who seems to know what Ya wants. But ever since you were little and I saw how quickly you learned Khemetian, I have wondered if Ya did not have a plan for you. When I came in yesterday and saw you and the princess, the first thought that came to me was that this was part of Ya's plan. So I want you to watch for the princess."

"Is she coming back?" I ask, excited.

"I think so."

"And if I see her, what should I do?"

Abba smiles. "I do not know, Almah. But *you* will."

Chapter Four

THE SOLDIERS RETURN each morning and begin searching at the house where they stopped the evening before. Because we know where they are going, we don't need to watch for them.

Instead I look for the princess. After getting water I walk toward Pi-Ramesses until I see the walls that surround the palace shining white in the sun like herons' wings. I think that somehow she will know I am there and come walking out. But she never does.

One morning on my way to stare at the white walls, I pass a small group of soldiers as they are about to start down another street. I pay them no attention. They must know by now that they are not going to find what they are looking for, especially since we know where they are going to search each day. Since that first day, neither they nor the crocodiles have found any children.

The soldiers have almost passed me, when suddenly, "You!"

I am startled and stop immediately. What have I done

now? I turn around slowly and am surprised to see a soldier smiling at me.

"Was it you I saw with Princess Meryetamun?" he asks me in Habiru. He speaks slowly and his accent is not very good.

I do not know what to say. Where did he see me with the princess? In Pi-Ramesses, or did the princess describe me to the soldiers and tell them to look for the girl who had insulted her? What am I supposed to do?

I look at him. Like all the soldiers, his chest is bare and gleams with a sweet-smelling oil, which shows off the hard muscles in his arms, shoulders, chest, and the smooth bare legs beneath his kilt. His eyes are painted gray and his hair is short.

"Yes," I say in Khemetian.

He looks as if he wants to ask me something but doesn't know if he should.

"What's your name?" He is still speaking Habiru.

"Almah."

"That's pretty."

"Thank you. What is your name?" I respond in Khemetian.

"Kakemour." Then he chuckles. "You speak Khemetian like a Khemetian," he says in his own language this time. "I speak Habiru like a Khemetian." He laughs.

I laugh with him.

"Do you think you will be seeing the princess again?" he asks suddenly.

I am surprised. Why is he asking me that? I start to say no, but then I remember what Abba said. "Maybe."

"Well, if you do, tell her that Kakemour said—" He stops. "Never mind."

I want to ask him what he was going to say. Then I blurt out, "Are you the one who wants to marry her?"

"How did you know? What did she say?" His voice is excited and eager. He laughs nervously.

"She said that she doesn't want to marry anyone. I don't, either," I add proudly.

Kakemour smiles sadly. "If she would say that to a stranger, then it must be true." He speaks softly as if he is talking to himself. Then, without another word, he turns and hurries to catch up with the rest of the soldiers.

The next morning I awake as usual when the black of the sky is turning gray. Since the night Ima left me on the roof to sleep alone, I have slept here. I don't want to be in the same room with her. Although I miss having Miryam and Aharon snuggle against me, Ima does not want them near me anymore.

I get up, and as I stretch I happen to look toward Pi-Ramesses, when I see them! Hundreds of soldiers running fast up the road.

I almost fall down the stairs. "Abba! Ima! Soldiers! Hundreds of them!" I do not wait for them to answer but grab Yekutiel's basket and take him from where he lies beside Ima. Aharon and Miryam awake and look at me curiously.

"What are you doing?" Ima says, reaching out for the baby.

I move away from her.

"Go, Almah! Quickly!" Abba says.

I run into the kitchen with Yekutiel and grab some bread and dates and am through the door, the sound of Ima wailing in my ears. I think I hear Abba right behind me, hurrying to warn as many of our neighbors as he can. The soldiers tricked us into thinking that they didn't care about finding any babies.

I hurry down the path to the river. Yekutiel has not made a sound, but he is strange that way. He almost never cries. Sometimes we wonder if there is something wrong with his voice.

When I reach the river, I settle myself at the lip of the embankment, where I can see the soldiers long before they see me. If I do see any, I'll put Yekutiel in the basket and hide it among the bulrushes. They are thick here and the basket is made of them. No one will ever find it unless he is looking for it. I hope.

For now I lay Yekutiel on my lap, facing me, his head resting lightly on my knees. The sun's warmth spreads over us. I would think it is a beautiful day if I couldn't hear the faint sounds of screaming and crying.

I hear someone coming and quickly put the baby in the basket, which is already hidden in the bulrushes. I scurry around a curve in the riverbank where I can hide and wait to see who it is. In a short while someone appears. It is Ima. She is looking frantically this way and that.

I stand up and hurry to her. "Ima!" I call, but quietly so only she can hear me.

"Almah! The baby! Where is he? I came to feed him."

When Ima sees how cleverly I hid the basket, she smiles at me. "You did well. Even I did not see it there."

I smile. I wish she said nice things to me more often.

She nurses him and then hurries back to the village. Yekutiel will sleep for many hours now.

The sun moves up the sky until it is directly overhead. I eat the bread and the dates I took as I hurried out. It is quiet now. I have not heard any crying and screaming from the village in a long while. I wonder if I can go back but decide to stay until Abba or Ima comes to get me.

Occasionally ducks land on the water and look at me. When they fly away I fear they are going to tell the soldiers where to find a Habiru baby.

The sun has started its downward journey when I hear someone coming. It is probably Ima coming to feed Yekutiel again, but I can't take any chances. I look quickly at the basket to be sure it is well hidden, then hurry to my hiding place around the curve of the river.

From the noise made by the leaves being brushed, I can tell there is more than one person. It must be soldiers! The sounds come closer and closer, and I cannot believe who steps into the clearing. The princess! It can't be! But it is. She looks different today. I do not know why until I notice that she is not wearing jewelry and, thus, does not sparkle in the sun. She is still beautiful. Behind her are two girls about my age who must be servants, because they are not wearing clothes.

The princess stands on the bank peering intently into the water. Suddenly she points. Oh no! She is pointing at the basket. How did she find it? Even Ima didn't see it. But the princess acted as if she knew where it was all along. But she couldn't have known. She couldn't have! What am I going to do?

I can hear her voice, but she is speaking so fast I do not understand a word. She is angry, though, and grabs one of the girls by the throat and then pushes her down. Both girls scramble down the embankment, get the basket, and set it at the princess's feet. She opens it. She is picking my brother up. I don't believe it. He is lying in her arms as if . . . as if . . . as if she is me or Ima. His head turns toward her breast and his little mouth puckers, moving back and forth. Then I see his mouth open as if he is going to cry out, and I spring up from my hiding place.

"Would the princess like my mother to nurse the child for her?" I call.

The princess turns. "Almah?" she exclaims. "Is this your brother? The one I thought I saw when I was at your house?"

What can I say? "Yes, Princess."

"Do not worry. He is safe with me. Taweret has given him to me."

" 'Taweret'?"

"She is the goddess who brings babies to women who are childless, as I am."

"But . . . but he is not yours," I say.

"He is unless you want the soldiers to kill him as they have killed so many today. Take me to your mother. The baby is hungry."

I feel sick. I have failed again. I saved my brother from the soldiers, but the princess says he is hers now. Abba and Ima will never trust me again.

Chapter Five

THE SOLDIERS ARE JUST entering my house when we come out of the marsh—the princess, her two servants, and me. Standing beside the door, Aharon and Miryam next to them, Abba's and Ima's eyes swell with fear as they see Yekutiel being carried by the princess. But as we come closer and they see how Yekutiel is making sounds at the princess and giggling when she tickles him under his chin, the fear is replaced by confusion. I am neither afraid nor confused. Just jealous. How dare he!

When the soldiers see the princess, they drop to their knees and bow. The only one who doesn't is the soldier who asked me about her yesterday: Kakemour.

"Meryetamun?" he asks, astonished to see her.

"Kakemour." The princess seems almost as surprised.

"I . . . I don't understand. What . . . what are you doing here?"

"The goddess Taweret has given me a child, as I'm sure you can see."

Kakemour frowns. "Be that as it may, you have placed

my men in an impossible position. How can we carry out the pharaoh's orders when his own daughter disobeys them? You are going against *maat*, 'divine order.'"

"How can I be going against *maat* when the goddess herself delivered this child into my hands?" the princess responds evenly.

Kakemour doesn't know what to say, and before he can think of anything, Yekutiel starts crying. Ima hurries to the princess and takes the baby from her. That only seems to make him cry harder and his tiny arms reach back for the princess as Ima takes him inside to nurse.

"Have you lost your mind?" Kakemour says to the princess, openly annoyed now.

"Do you know to whom you are speaking?" the princess replies sharply, her eyes narrowing. "You may be the son of Intef, the *tjat*, prime minister, to Pharaoh, and the future *tjat*, but even then I will be Meryetamun, daughter of Ramesses the Great!"

Kakemour turns red and bows. "Forgive me, Princess, favorite daughter of the Lord of the Two Lands, son of Amon-Re." His voice is sarcastic, then it softens as he says, "I thought you were Meryetamun, my oldest friend, my dearest friend, and the woman I want to marry."

Their voices are quiet, but I can still hear them. The princess's face softens. "Even when we were children, you wanted me to be only Meryetamun. You wanted to forget what I cannot forget. I am not just Meryetamun. I am also Pharaoh's daughter."

"Which means that you more than anyone cannot disobey his orders!"

Anger returns to her voice. "And have I stopped you from killing babies? No! Have I told you not to kill anymore? No! What order have I disobeyed, Kakemour?" She stops and suddenly tears are in her eyes. "You kill babies and still want me to marry you?"

Kakemour turns a deep red, and when he speaks his words stun me. "Why do you care? They are only Habiru babies. The way these people breed, they will outnumber us before we know it. I do not have the luxury of being able to choose which orders of the pharaoh I will or will not obey. I am only the son of Intef, the *tjat*. The pharaoh orders, I obey."

"My father will not go against what the goddess Taweret has done. My father may even believe, as I do, that the goddess gave me this child as a sign she wants the killing to stop. It is not every day, Kakemour, that the daughter of Pharaoh holds a Habiru baby in her arms. And you saw how the child cried for me when I gave him to his mother. What would your father counsel you to do? Would he tell you to kill the daughter of the pharaoh so you can carry out your orders? And exactly how would you make Ramesses understand why you murdered his favorite daughter? And how do you think he would respond?"

Kakemour looks down, his face twisted in confusion. "All right. We will stop searching for today, and we will escort you back to the palace. As you know, my father, the pharaoh, and your mother, Queen Nefertari, are on their way to Opet for the festival to mark the inundation.

However, Queen Asetnefret, the Second Royal Wife, remains. We will see what she says about all this."

I understand their words but not what they're talking about. Abba looks at me, and I can tell he is anxious to know what has been said. I don't think he is going to like the part about some goddess giving my brother to the princess. What if she is serious? My brother would go to live behind those white walls. But that's where I want to live.

"Come," the princess says to me. "I want to meet your mother."

She follows me into the dark house, through the kitchen and the middle room, and into the front one, where Ima sits on the floor nursing Yekutiel. Aharon and Miryam crouch at her side, looking like the broken wings of a bird. Abba has followed the princess and me into the room and sits down behind Ima.

"You will translate?" the princess asks me.

"I'll try."

The princess kneels on the floor in front of Ima and Abba. Ima looks down at Yekutiel. "I am Princess Meryetamun, daughter of Pharaoh, Lord of the Two Lands, son of the god Amon-Re. Please do not be afraid. I do not mean you or anyone in your family any harm. When I came here some weeks ago, I was upset. Just that morning I had learned from a friend, the soldier I was speaking with outside, that the army would be coming here to kill your newborn sons. I couldn't understand why I was so upset. Like all Khemetians, I had always thought of the

Habiru as uncivilized—with their ugly language, and all that hair your women have on their heads, and the men with hair on their heads and faces. To us a body must be cleaned of hair from head to foot to be attractive and to honor our gods.

"So I was surprised at how distressed I was that a man who wanted to marry me was going to kill babies, even if they were Habiru."

She stops and waits for me to catch up. Ima is looking at her now. Abba's eyes have never left her face.

"I was so upset that I ran from the palace. I didn't have a destination in mind. I needed to get away. I did not know I was in Goshen until I began seeing men and women with their own hair. Then I saw the crocodile kill the baby."

Her voice trembles and she stops. She bites her lip as if trying not to cry. Taking a deep breath, she continues. "Well, I did not actually see it. I saw the crocodile, and I saw the basket and the baby inside. And I saw the crocodile swimming toward the basket. That is when I fainted. If Almah had not been there, it is possible a crocodile might have dragged me into the water."

She turns and looks at me, smiling. "Your daughter is the first person I've ever met who is not afraid of me. I feel like she is more my sister than any of my own. She even dared tell me the truth. People usually tell me only what they think I want to hear.

"If I had wanted to harm you, I would have told the soldiers you were hiding the babies in baskets among the bulrushes on the river. I could have directed them here to your house, where I knew there was a baby. Instead, ever since I was here, I have thought of little else than that baby the crocodile killed. If I had seen the basket sooner, or if I had been more brave, perhaps I could have saved him. But I didn't do anything. Nothing. I didn't even scream. Maybe that would have frightened the crocodile away. I didn't even think to pick up a rock and throw it. I did nothing.

"I was so afraid the soldiers would find your baby. Every morning, when I woke up, the first thing I thought of was Almah and this house and whether your baby was safe. I knew that if I did nothing, the soldiers or a crocodile might eventually find him. This morning I couldn't tolerate it anymore, couldn't tolerate not knowing what had happened to him. So I came to find out.

"The soldiers were just a street away when I got here, and I knew they would be coming to this house soon. I am convinced the goddess led me to the path and the baby. How else could I have found it? When I held him and saw how he looked at me, I knew. He is my son. I want to take him to live with me in the palace and raise him there. Of course, he is still your son, too, but please! I must have this child to raise as my own. Because he is still nursing, would you come and live in the palace and nurse him until he is weaned? And Almah must come to be our translator—and my little sister." The princess looks at me and smiles.

I can't believe what I am hearing. But as I tell Ima, I try to keep any excitement out of my voice. If Ima knows how much I want to go, she will say no. When I finish telling her what the princess has said, I expect Ima to start screaming and yelling. But she doesn't. She looks at the princess. Then she turns and looks over her shoulder at Abba. Yekutiel has finished nursing and lies in the crook of her arm, making little baby sounds and moving his legs. But he is not looking at Ima. He is looking at the princess. I have never seen him this lively. It is as if he has just been born.

The room is so still. Aharon and Miryam look at me, their faces wondering what is wrong. Then Abba asks me in Habiru, "How did she find you and Yekutiel?"

The princess looks at me, expecting me to translate, but I do not. "She said she followed the path through the marsh."

"No!" Ima cuts in. "If a person does not know the path is there, they would not see it. Who led her there?"

"I do not know, Ima. I did not tell her," I add quickly.

"No one is accusing you," Ima says softly.

She is still for a long time. Finally she looks at Abba. If I didn't know him so well, I would not have seen the faint nod of his head. But I do not know what he is saying yes to. I understand only when Ima hands Yekutiel to the princess, tears in her eyes, and says, "My husband said some days ago that Ya, the one god, would use you to stop the killing. In exchange it seems that Ya wants you to have our son."

I do not translate.

"Tell her!" Ima snaps at me.

I do so, afraid the princess is going to start talking about that Taweret goddess. What does it matter if it is

Taweret or Ya who saves my brother? All I care is that Ya and Taweret seem to be in agreement.

"Almah?" It is the princess. "Tell your mother she can bring the two little children. I know it would be hard for them to be separated from her."

I translate, and I am surprised when Ima replies, angrily, "No! I will not give all of my children away. Aharon is with his father all day. A neighbor will take care of Miryam."

Although my wish has come true, I am sorry to be leaving. I will miss watching the sunrise, carrying water from the river, watching Abba pray in the morning, and talking with him before he goes to work. Suddenly I am afraid this is all a mistake, that something is changing forever.

All too soon we are walking to Pi-Ramesses. I wish I could have talked to Abba and heard what he thinks is going to happen, but there was no time. Now there is only silence. I am between the princess—Yekutiel in her arms—and Ima. Abba walks on the other side of Ima. Kakemour is beside the princess, and behind him, the soldiers. On both sides of the road people stand and watch. They, too, are silent.

I try to see us through their eyes. It is not surprising that no one knows what to say. Who has ever seen Pharaoh's daughter walking with Habiru and carrying a Habiru baby? Everyone seems to know that something important is happening, but they do not know what it is. Neither do we who are doing it.

We enter Pi-Ramesses and, after a short distance, turn

up the long walkway of painted stones as smooth as glass that lead to the white walls. However, as we approach the tall doors with the lotus and papyrus painted on them, they swing open. The princess draws in her breath sharply. Standing there is a tall woman wearing a long dress as white and soft as heron feathers. The princess stops. Abba, Ima, and I stop, also. I hear noise behind me and turn to see the soldiers drop to their knees and bow. Kakemour walks past us, however, and only when he is standing directly in front of the woman does he drop to his knees and bend the upper half of his body to the ground. Then he rises and the woman motions him to stand beside her.

"Who is she?" Ima asks me in a whisper.

"I think she is Queen Asetnefret."

She steps out from the shadows into the waning light of the setting sun. Beside me I hear the princess breathing hard, as if she is out of breath from running, though she has been standing still.

"And what do you think you're doing? You would bring a Habiru child into the house of Ramesses?" the queen says in a loud voice.

Ima pinches my arm, wanting to know what she said, but I am afraid to speak.

"Just because you are Ramesses's favorite daughter, it does not mean you can disobey his orders. Do you want me to send word of your impudence to Ramesses?"

"If you wish," the princess responds, her voice almost too soft to be heard.

The queen laughs, but there is no laughter in her

voice or eyes. "Oh, you don't think Ramesses will punish his darling daughter? You are wrong! However, if you give me the child, Ramesses need not hear anything about this."

Ima grabs my arm and shakes it. "What's going on? What did she say?"

I do not answer. Ima looks at Abba. He does not look at her.

"Give me the child!" the queen repeats.

The princess is so still, I wonder if she has died but has not fallen to the ground.

The queen looks at Kakemour and nods. Kakemour begins walking toward us. He is coming to take Yekutiel!

Ima understands now what is about to happen, but before Ima can do anything, the princess says in a strong voice, "You will have to kill me first! And explain that to my father. Even his Second Royal Wife would not be able to convince him it was necessary to kill his favorite daughter. This child is my son, given to me by the goddess Taweret. I do not disobey my father. I obey the goddess."

Kakemour doesn't seem to know whether to keep coming forward, stop where he is, or go back and stand beside the queen. He stops and looks at the queen. I don't know who this Taweret is, but every time the princess mentions her name, it makes a difference.

The queen laughs again. It is a sound you wish you had not heard. "So, this Habiru boy was given to you by Taweret."

"Yes!"

51

"Then what is his name?"

The queen has obviously said something very important because Kakemour smiles and the soldiers suddenly start talking excitedly among themselves.

"What did she say?" Ima wants to know, concerned.

"The queen asked the princess for Yekutiel's name."

"Then tell the princess. Tell her!"

I turn to the princess and whisper, "His name is—"

"Silence!" she responds harshly, shocking me.

"I'm only trying to help," I insist.

"You aren't."

"What is going on? What is going on?" Ima wants to know.

Before I can say I don't know, I hear the princess announce in a loud voice, "His name is Thutmosis."

Everyone gasps. The queen stares at the princess, and then, without a word, she bows her head and stands to the side. Kakemour does the same and the princess walks forward into the palace, Yekutiel asleep in her arms. Ima and I follow. As I reach the door, I turn around to see Abba. In the darkness he is only a shape among many.

Chapter Six

ONCE A WEEK—every ten days—Abba comes to visit and brings Aharon and Miryam to see Ima. We meet them outside the white walls because he is not allowed inside the Women's Palace. Aharon and Miryam sit with Ima and Mosis, as we call him now, on the grass beneath the shade of a tree. Abba and I sit a distance away, under another tree, where I tell him everything. Well, almost everything.

Abba is glad I'm happy, but I think he's afraid of my being too happy. So I don't tell him that I never want to leave! One of Ima's many stories is about Adam and Chava, the first man and woman. They lived in Gan Eden, a beautiful garden where they never had to work and could have anything they wanted. That is just a story. Living here is real!

"The Women's Palace is so big that when I stand in the hallway outside the princess's suite, I cannot see to the other end. That's where Queen Nefertari lives with her other children, but they're not here now. They're away doing something with the pharaoh. The princess has her own suite because she is an adult now. She has fifteen rooms, each one bigger than our house! The suite is on the second floor. Queen Asetnefret and her children live on the first floor, but they don't talk to us and we don't talk to them."

Abba smiles. "I see."

"I have my own room, Abba."

"A room just for you?"

"A room just for me! It has a balcony, which is like a porch up in the air. Beautiful flowers and plants hang from it, and every day a servant waters them. I sit out there and can see the lake. Can you believe there's a huge lake behind those walls? And from my balcony I can see a pyramid in the distance."

There is so much I want to tell him, and it all tries to come rushing out at once. "And guess what, Abba?" I say, lowering my voice. Without waiting for him to ask "What?" I hurry on before I get too embarrassed. "The bathroom is *inside*! And in the bathroom there's a big smooth stone that slants down, and you lie on it naked and a servant pours water over you and the water goes out through a hole in the floor. The princess says a person must be clean all the time and that body odor is against something called *maat*. The princess takes a bath at least three times a day. And she lets me take baths whenever I want."

"Oh really?" He smiles. "And do you?"

"Three times a day—like her," I say proudly.

I also tell him about my bed! I didn't know such a thing existed. It is four long pieces of wood fastened together to make a square, inside of which are strings that have been plaited together like a mat. Big cushions lie on top of the strings. "And that's what I sleep on. It is so-o-o soft. The first few nights I was afraid I would sink so far down, someone would have to pull me out. Now I don't care if I ever get out."

I expected Abba to chuckle, or at least smile, but he does not respond at all. I'm sorry I said that last part about not ever wanting to get out. "Ima still sleeps on the floor. She says she doesn't want to get used to anything in the house of Pharaoh."

"Your mother is smart."

Now it is my turn not to say anything.

I want to tell him about the princess's huge bed, which has feet that look like a little ugly man. His head is like a lion's, but he is wearing a crown of feathers. He has huge ears, bowed legs, a tail, and he is sticking his tongue out. The princess calls him Bes, the dwarf god, and says he is a friend to women and brings happiness to a house. Even though he's ugly, there's something about him that I like. The princess wanted to give me a necklace with a likeness of him on it, but I didn't take it.

I don't say anything to Abba about all the silence, either. At first it was hard to go to sleep without Abba snoring, Ima grinding her teeth, and the crocodiles roaring. Now I fall asleep and wake up to silence, and I am reluctant to get up because I don't want to wound it.

"I have never seen you like this," Abba remarks. "It is almost as if you have not been happy until now."

It is true, and when I don't deny it, it is as if I nodded.

But I am afraid the princess will send me away in disgust because I am so ignorant. The first meal we had I stood with my mouth open, staring at the gold plates and cups. Until the servants started putting food on the plates and pouring wine into the cups, I didn't know we were going to actually use them. And the food! Every day I can eat antelope, roast duck, roast goose, gazelle, quail, pigeon, or porcupine. There are sweet onions, garlic, leeks, and olives, and the juiciest dates and figs I have ever seen— and something called coconuts, which have milk inside and a white fleshy pulp. They are so good!

Ima says Ya doesn't want us to eat all those things. Maybe Ya isn't as hungry as I am. I didn't know until I moved here, but I think I have been hungry since I was born. I eat so much and it is never enough. When I'm not eating, I'm sleeping, and when I'm not doing either of those, I'm taking a bath or wandering around the palace looking at the walls, which are painted with scenes of marshes and birds flying and fish swimming. It is as if all the beauty of outside has been brought inside, so that when you're inside you can also be outside. I can't believe there are people who can paint animals and trees and fish and make them look real.

My favorite place, though, is the garden, which has trees and grass, baboons, monkeys, and all kinds of birds. In the center is a big lake surrounded by tall palm trees. At the far end is a building with a ramp that extends into the water, a pavilion, the princess called it. Queen Aset-nefret likes to sit there in the afternoon with her children.

Ima doesn't like it here, even though the princess has told the servants to treat us as if we are members of her family, to bring us food and drink whenever we want, to walk behind Ima wherever she goes, and to hold a large round fan on a long pole over her head to shade her from the sun—and when she sits down, to fan her from behind. But Ima doesn't want servants doing anything for her. "Ya did not make some people to serve others," she said. "He made us to serve him. I cannot do that if someone is serving me."

I could.

Yet even though she doesn't like it here, she has been asking me to tell her the Khemetian words for things, and the princess has been asking me how to say things in Habiru. I'm afraid if Ima learns Khemetian and the princess learns Habiru, they won't need me anymore and I'll have to return to Goshen. I will kill myself before I go back. I don't say this to Abba, either.

"The soldiers have stayed away," Abba tells me. "You saved our people," he adds.

I shake my head, though I am pleased he thinks so. "I didn't do anything."

"You were not afraid of the princess."

"But I didn't know what that would lead to," I respond.

"No. But Ya did. If you had not gone to the princess when she fainted, Ya would not have been able to do anything. You made it possible for him to use the princess and stop the killing."

I nod as if I understand, but I don't. I'm not even sure I believe in Ya. I'm not sure I ever did. Although I am sad when it is time for Abba to leave, I am also glad. Things are not the same. Aharon and Miryam look at me as if I am a stranger, and when I try to talk to them or play with them, they shrink away from me as if I smell bad. Even Abba looks at me as if he is not sure who I am anymore.

The next day Ima and I are sitting in the garden. We are together now more than ever and I am getting tired of listening to her stories about our ancestors, Avraham and Sarah, Yitzchak and Rivka, and Yaakov and all his wives. I've heard these stories all my life and know them by heart.

"I don't want you to forget where you came from. I don't want you to forget your people," she keeps telling me, her face pinched as if her thoughts hurt her, her shoulders hunched as if she is carrying something heavy inside—too heavy for her thin body.

"I have never seen you so happy," she says.

I am not sure what to say. I am very, very happy but am afraid she will get angry if I say so.

"You and Mosis," she adds, the foreign name said as if there is something bitter on her tongue.

"It is very nice here," I say, keeping pleasure out of my voice.

She is silent again. Then, "Do you believe this Taweret gave your brother to the princess?"

Why is she asking me? Is this a trick? If I say yes, I'm in trouble. If I don't say anything, I'm also in trouble. "I . . . I don't know."

There is another long pause. I am afraid to breathe. But when she finally speaks, her voice is softer than I have ever heard it. "It is odd to give birth to a child but never feel the child is yours. Aharon, Miryam—they are my children. I know it without having to think about it. But you and Mosis? When I was carrying you, it was like you were in me but not of me. But you were my first and I thought maybe that's how it is. But with Aharon and Miryam, it was so different. When they were inside me, I talked and sang to them. I never talked or sang to you. Even then it was as if you were someplace I could not reach you. I knew who Aharon and Miryam were by how they moved in my belly. But you kicked and punched me, especially when I tried to sleep. I asked Ya if you were angry. He said no. Mosis was silent. I wondered sometimes if he was dead because he seldom moved. When he was born he did not cry. You seemed to cry only when I came near. I would pick you up and you would kick at me and beat on my arms with your tiny fists. But Amram would just lay his hand on your belly and you would be quiet. When he held you, you did not make a sound. I wondered why you hated me so."

Ima is staring at the lake, but her eyes seem to be looking at something deep in her memory. She has never spoken to me like this, and even though I am sure she is going to say something to hurt me, I don't want her to stop. I wonder if she is waiting for me to apologize for doing things I don't remember, or if she wants me to tell her that I don't hate her. I could tell her that and it would be true. But not all the truth. It is not that I hate her. I don't think I like her—and that's worse, I think.

But before I can figure out what to say, she continues. "You are almost a woman, Almah. Amram doesn't think I understand that. But of course I do. I am a woman. Why wouldn't I understand? But your father loves you more than is good for either of you. Sometimes I think he loves you more than he loves me. He thinks I hate you. You do, too. Don't you?"

She looks at me for the first time. I want to lie, but I blush and she can see the truth.

She opens her arms. Hesitantly I move closer, and she puts her arms around me and holds me tightly. I am trying hard not to cry.

"I am sorry, my daughter. I do not hate you. I love you. You are my firstborn and therefore you will always be special. But I am frightened. You are my daughter, my firstborn, and yet I do not know you. You have never needed me except when I nursed you. A mother likes to feel needed, likes to feel that her children will come to her with questions and problems. You never have. You've always gone to your father. You need him. You even need the princess. I see you look at her as you have never looked at me. And now there is Mosis, who cries when I pick him up and smiles when the princess holds him. I have a son and cannot call him by the name I gave him. That night I did not know. If I had known that the princess was giving him a name, and her doing so gave her power over him, that she was naming him for an idol that has the head of an ibis, I think I would have died before I let her do it."

"But he is named for the god of wisdom," I protest, "the god who loves truth."

Ima looks at me with disgust. "There is no god but Ya!" Then she sighs. "Often I have wondered why he gave you and Mosis to me. I've asked him if he didn't make a mistake. And now, when I see how happy you are here among idolaters, when I see how happy Mosis is with the princess, I am glad I believe in Ya as deeply as I do. Otherwise I would think your true mother was this Taweret."

She starts crying, then gets up and hurries into the palace. I want to run after her and tell her there was no mistake. Just because you're born to someone, it doesn't mean you belong to them.

THE NEXT MORNING Ima has just finished nursing Mosis. As she hands him to the princess, she says, "I gave birth to him, but Ya wants him to be your son."

I look at her sharply, my face asking if she really wants me to translate that. And I don't understand. Yesterday she was saying Taweret gave us to the princess.

"Tell her," Ima orders me.

I do. The princess looks at Ima, a quizzical expression on her face. "How do you know?"

"I prayed to Ya most of the night. I am not happy that my son and my daughter are happier in the palace of an idolater than with their mother. But Ya told me that this is what he wants. I do not understand. But just as our father, Avraham, obeyed when Ya told him to sacrifice his favorite son, I will obey now."

"Who is this Ya you're always talking about, Yocheved?" the princess asks. "What does he look like?"

"He cannot be seen," Ima says.

"Then how do you know he exists or where he is? There are statues of Ramesses all over Khemet so that wherever the people are, they can see their god."

"Statues can break," Ima responds, a sly smile on her lips. "The invisible god is everywhere at the same time and is eternal. It was Ya who sent you to Goshen."

The princess laughs lightly. "That's ridiculous."

"Is it? Think about it. You had never been there in your life. Yet you just happen into Goshen on the day and at the exact time a crocodile killed a baby someone had hidden on the river. You fainted exactly when Almah happened to be watching. Any other Habiru girl would have left you there. My people do not think too highly of Khemetians. But you just happened to faint in front of the one Habiru girl who speaks your language fluently. I say all this was the work of Ya."

"It *is* odd," the princess admits reluctantly. "But why can't you believe in this Ya of yours and our gods, too?"

"Your country is great and powerful, isn't it?"

"Yes, it is."

"Many peoples pay tribute to Pharaoh and bow to him as a god."

"Yes."

"Except the Habiru. We are the only ones who do not

bow to Pharaoh. If we were not sure that Ya exists and is greater than Pharaoh, we would have bowed our heads to your father many, many years ago. Your father is merely a man who will one day die. Like me. Like you. How can someone be a god if his end is the same as mine?"

"I never thought of that," the princess responds, as if what Ima said made sense. I want to tell her that a god who cannot die does not know what it is like to be a person, cannot understand us. Why is the princess looking at Ima as if she is wonderful?

Chapter Seven

"RAMESSES IS RETURNING!"

Queen Asetnefret's loud voice in the main room of the suite wakes me. Ima comes in from her room next door, her eyes asking me what is going on. Whispering, I translate.

"But why?" the princess responds. "The Festival of Opet has scarcely begun."

Asetnefret laughs that laugh that makes me think about preparing to die. "I sent word to him that you are out of control and disobeying his orders. It seems he is sufficiently distressed that he is coming back immediately. If I were you I'd get this Habiru woman, her daughter, and that baby out of here today. If they aren't here, especially the baby, Ramesses might forgive you. Let me put it this way. I can guarantee you that Ramesses will forgive you."

"What're you talking about?" The princess's voice is angry. "You talk like Ramesses does whatever you say."

"You are naive, Meryetamun. Just because your mother, Nefertari, is always at Pharaoh's side, it does not mean she has influence. Ramesses likes beautiful women, and even I will admit that your mother is the most beautiful woman I have ever seen. If I were Pharaoh, I would want a thing of beauty by my side, too. However, when he needs to talk about important matters, he talks to me. It was I who persuaded him that the Habiru were becoming too numerous and could not be trusted. Ramesses is too busy bringing new wives into his harem and fathering children to know when his reign is threatened."

"I *knew* it! I knew my father would not have thought of something like that. I knew it!"

Queen Asetnefret says something else, but I can't hear it, and then it is silent, except for the sound of the princess crying softly. The queen must have left. Ima and I walk quietly along the corridor and into the main room. The princess sits on a couch, her legs tucked beneath her, her head down. Ima sits down next to her and puts her arms around her as she has never put them around me. I do not want to look. Then I think, maybe the princess's mother will love me like my mother loves the princess.

I go into the room next to the princess's bedroom, the one where she keeps the jars of colors she puts on her eyes and lips and cheeks. I sit down on the stool before a low table where the jars are arranged neatly in a row. On the table also is a mirror whose handle is in the shape of the naked body of a woman with long, beautiful legs. Her arms curve over her head to form a circle, inside of which is a disk of pure gold that shines like the sun. But her arms are not just arms. They are also wings with long feathers, each one carved from gold. (*"Her name is Eset, but*

65

we also call her Mut-netjer, the Mother of the Gods. Khemetians love her more than they do any other goddess. She is selfless. She has great powers, but she uses them for others. Every morning, when I hold this mirror, it is like reminding myself to be like her. I suppose it was Eset who led me to return to Goshen and try to save your brother.")

I should not be in here by myself, though the princess has never said I couldn't. Every morning I sit on the floor and watch as the two servants put the colors on her face and rub the sweet-smelling oils into her body. More than once she has asked me if I want color around my eyes, or maybe a tiny bit of red on my lips. I shake my head, but my heart is pounding—*yes, yes, yes!*

I look at the mirror and Eset almost seems alive. I know the mirror was made by someone, that Eset is not really alive, but looking at her makes me hope that when I am a woman, my breasts will be proud and full like hers. How could someone make something so beautiful—and from gold—if it were not alive somewhere? I do not know if Eset really exists, but the feelings I have when looking at her are real. This is how I wanted to feel those mornings when I stood naked by the river and faced the sun. Maybe that's what Eset and Taweret and all the other gods and goddesses do. They help us see our feelings. They help us see who we are and who we can be.

I touch her foot lightly. The gold is cool and hard. I let my fingers go slowly and lightly up and down the legs, and then to the round breasts, the arms, and along the feathers. Over and over my fingers caress her. Maybe if I touch her long enough, I, too, will be able to stand naked and beautiful, and then my arms will become wings.

66

I don't mean to, but my hand curls around the handle and I raise the mirror and am startled by the face I see. The girl looking back at me has long, curly dark hair. Her eyes are dark, also, and shaped like narrow almonds. The nose is also narrow, but it is her lips that stand out. It is as though her face decided to wait and find all its expression in lips that are large and full. I do not know what to think. It is different looking at myself here than seeing my reflection in the river. I think I may be beautiful. Or I could be.

I take the lids from the jars and look at the colors inside. They are shiny and oily. The princess puts red on her cheeks, but what would it be like to wear the sky on your face and to put the color of blood around your eyes? (*"Wearing paint around the eyes protects them from the sun as well as makes one look more beautiful."*) I am afraid I will get paint in my eyes, but what if I put a little red on my lips? Just a little. Not enough even that anyone would notice.

I put my little finger lightly into the red paint and touch it to my bottom lip and rub it in all the way across. I hold up the mirror. My lip looks as if it is on fire! I put a little more paint on my finger and rub it across my top lip. I look in the mirror again. My lips look like the sunset. I take more paint and rub it into my cheeks. My face looks like a flower!

I take off my dress and stand stiffly, my legs together, and raise my arms above my head in a circle. I wish I could see myself, wish I could see if I look like Eset. I think I do because I don't feel like Almah anymore, and maybe that is why I do not hear the door open.

"What are you doing?"

I drop my arms immediately, hurriedly pick my dress up from the floor and slip it over my head. "Just . . . just pretending," I say to Ima, my voice barely audible.

"You look beautiful," the princess says. She is smiling. "I knew you would."

I want to smile back, but Ima's eyes are holding me as if she has her hands around my throat. "You look like a Khemetian whore!" she spits at me. "What do you think your father would say if he saw you like this?"

I cannot look at her and my eyes drop to the floor. But then I remember Eset. I remember the feeling she gave me and I don't want to lose it. I force myself to look up. Ima's face is angry. It hurts to be looked at with anger.

"Wipe that paint off your face. I am sending you back to Goshen!"

I don't know what to do. I look at the princess. Her face is like a question mark. I translate what Ima said, then add, "I think I'll die if I have to go back there."

"Then stay," the princess responds simply. "It would be good for your brother to grow up knowing his oldest sister."

"What did she say?" Ima asks angrily.

I hesitate.

"What did you say to her and what did she say?" Ima asks again, more angry now.

"She said she will need help raising Mosis and it would be better for him if it came from his own sister rather than one of the servants."

I have never lied to Ima. I have never needed to. Until

now. Ima is looking me directly in the eye. I stare back at her. If she would let me be myself, I wouldn't have to lie.

It is Ima whose eyes waver first. She looks away, then down toward the floor. Quickly she raises her head and stares at me, but I do not blink or look away. I stare back at her as if my eyes are suns. She blinks and her eyes waver again, then shift to the side. I can't believe it! I have won! Ima will never be able to hurt me again!

Chapter Eight

THE PHARAOH HAS RETURNED! The princess and Queen Asetnefret went to the big palace yesterday, and neither has come back. A high wall with a gate separates the Women's Palace from the palace where the pharaoh lives. I went to the gate, but the guards stopped me, wanting to know who I was and what I wanted and what was a Habiru doing there?

With the princess gone, I have no one to talk to. Ima has not spoken to me since that morning. I sit in the garden hoping to see the princess returning. Why has she been gone so long? She is pleading with Pharaoh not to send us back to Goshen. Will I be sitting here in the garden next month, feeling the warmth of the sun on my skin, watching the baboons in the trees and the geese on the lake? Or will I be dead? Those are the only choices.

Will Abba understand if I never return to Goshen? Will he understand why I need a goddess, why I need to be able to see that goddess and touch her? How can I make him understand when I do not?

"Almah?"

The sound of someone calling my name startles me. I look around. It is Kakemour! I quickly get to my feet. There is so much about Khemetian ways I do not know. Do you bow to a soldier? Am I supposed to call him by a special title?

"Oh, you don't have to get up," he says kindly. "May I sit down?"

I hesitate. Why is he here? Has he come to send me back to Goshen? Is he going to kill Mosis this time? But he is being nice to me. Why?

"I can understand that you might not want to sit with me. I . . . I was not exactly friendly the last time we saw each other. If you let me sit down, perhaps I can explain. Or at least apologize."

Slowly I sit back down and motion him to sit down also. He looks so different without a spear in his hand, without all the soldiers around, without Queen Asetnefret giving orders. I hope I am not being rude, but I look at his face and I like that I can see his skin and how smooth it is. I can even see the line of his jaw, and it is strong. Abba says Ya wants the Habiru to cover their faces with hair. Why would Ya care about hair? Suddenly I am aware that I have never been so close to a man so young and handsome. He smells like flowers and his skin glistens like the sun on the river. I want to put my hand on his chest.

"I don't know what happened to me that day," he says softly. "Before we went I thought I was going to enjoy it. Meryetamun and I sat right here on this bench a few weeks before, and I told her the pharaoh had ordered us to kill all the newborn male children in Goshen. I didn't think she would care. But she was furious. She ran away and ended up in Goshen, where you found her.

"It was my first assignment as a soldier. I wanted to do well and make my father proud of me. Make the pharaoh proud of me. I said some ugly and hateful things about your people and I'm sorry. I hope you will forgive me. I did not want the other soldiers to think I was weak. But I hated what we did there. I hope you believe me when I say that I did not kill any babies. Please tell the princess that for me."

"But you didn't stop anyone else from killing them," I say flatly. "And what would you have done if Queen Aset-nefret had told you to kill my brother?"

His head drops. "I . . . I don't know. I think I probably would have obeyed. I could not have gone against *maat*. I'm sorry."

"I am, too," I say quietly.

"At least you will tell the princess for me that I did not kill any babies. She's going to need a friend now."

"What do you mean?"

"You don't know?"

"Know what?"

"Her mother, Queen Nefertari, died suddenly in Opet. That is why the pharaoh has returned."

"Oh no!" I exclaim. "I am so sorry."

"So am I. She was a wonderful woman. I don't think any woman has ever been loved as much as the pharaoh loved her. My father says he is not sure if the pharaoh himself will survive the shock of not having Queen Nefertari beside him every day. They were inseparable."

"Your father is *tjat?*"

"Yes. And I will become *tjat* when he dies."

"Yosef was *tjat*," I put in.

"Who?"

"Yosef. My mother tells stories about Yosef. He was one of our ancestors who became the second most powerful man in Khemet."

"Psontenpa'anh."

"Who?"

"That is the name of your Yosef in Khemetian. You should be careful not to tell your mother's stories to a Khemetian."

"Why? Maybe if people knew the story of Yosef they would be nicer to the Habiru."

"Maybe if you knew the true story you would understand why we do not like Habiru."

"What do you mean?" I ask, curious and afraid.

"Many years ago a people called the Amu lived among us. Over time their numbers increased until there were almost as many of them as us, and they gained power. Their leader called himself Pharaoh, but he was a false pharaoh who destroyed our temples and enslaved our people. Your Yosef was *tjat* to this pharaoh. Your Yosef helped him enslave our people by making them sell their bodies into slavery in exchange for grain during a long famine. That is why now, when the pharaoh saw that there were more and more Habiru, he became afraid that they would take over again as they did when they joined with the Amu."

"But we do not want to rule your country. We only want to be allowed to go to the land Ya promised us."

Kakemour nods. "I know. But we remember what happened before."

I am angry. "Well, I don't believe your story. It's not true!"

"Well, it is as true for us as your story is for you. It is what we believe, and that is why we do not trust Habiru." Kakemour gets up. "I have to go. Please tell Meryetamun that if she needs a friend now, I am here."

I nod. As I watch him walk quickly away, I wish there were someone I could talk to. How can two stories be true? Or is something true only because a lot of people believe it?

Chapter Nine

I AM SORRY I NEVER MET Queen Nefertari. She must have been a wonderful mother, because the princess has done almost nothing but cry for a week now. She wails and screams and sobs until she is exhausted. Then she sleeps for a little while, only to awake and begin crying again. Ima is with her almost all the time, holding her, talking to her, singing to her. They do not ask me to translate and I do not want to.

Sadness fills the palace like the waters of the river that have spread over the land. Everyone walks slowly and speaks softly. Many have tears in their eyes, especially the servants. People tell me how beautiful and kind and wonderful she was, as if by speaking of her they can bring her back to life. By the way they have been talking to me about her, I think people are getting used to me and are seeing me as one of them. Maybe that is because I paint my cheeks and lips every morning, but not my eyes—yet.

I am sitting in the garden and suddenly everything is still. The servants working by the lake are looking toward the long pathway leading to the gate between this palace and the big one. Suddenly everyone drops to their knees and their bodies bend over until their heads touch the ground.

I turn to see what is happening, and when I see him come through the gate, I slip from the bench and drop to my knees, also. I do not intend to. It just happens. I have never seen him, but I know who it is! I should bow, but I don't want to because I have never seen a god.

The pharaoh is tall and wears a headdress colored blue like early morning. From the center of it extends the head of a cobra. The bottom is covered by a broad band of gold. His face is long and narrow, and the line of his jaw looks as strong as an arm. His eyes are set deep back in his head like a hawk's. He is wearing a long white robe and beneath it a garment of yellow. Around his neck is a large necklace of blue, red, and yellow jewels.

He must be going to see the princess. No. He is turning up the stone walk that leads this way! I know I should bow or run or do something, but I cannot move and I cannot take my eyes off him. Only when he looks directly into my eyes does my body let go, and my head touches the ground.

"You must be Almah." I hear a soft and low voice.

I raise my head but do not get to my feet. I do not know what to say. He did not ask me if I was Almah. He knew. Why would the pharaoh know who I am?

He stares at me with small, piercing dark eyes. Then he smiles. It is a sad smile, but a smile, nonetheless. "I understand now," he says, looking over his shoulder at the two men standing a short distance behind him. It is

Kakemour, and next to him, a small man who must be the *tjat*, Kakemour's father. For some reason Kakemour is smiling at me.

"You will sit with me?" the pharaoh says.

I am speechless. The pharaoh wants me to sit with him? As I get to my feet I wonder if he has come in person to send me back to Goshen because the princess would not do it. But if he were going to send me away, he would not have smiled at me.

The pharaoh sits on the bench and beckons me to sit beside him. Two tall male servants arrange themselves behind him, and with their long-handled feathered fans, create a gentle breeze. "Come," he says to me.

I get up and sit timidly at the edge of the bench. Kakemour stands beside me while his father stands on the other side, next to the pharaoh. I dare to look at Pharaoh. He does not look like a god. Just a very sad man. His eyes are red and puffy like the princess's, and his body sags into itself as if he is too weary to hold it up.

"I am sorry about the death of the queen," I offer quietly.

He looks at me, but I cannot tell if I should have said that. His gaze returns to the lake. "This was *her* favorite place to sit," he says.

"Oh. I didn't know." Is he offended to find me sitting where his dead wife sat? "It . . . it is very peaceful here," I add, seeking to explain.

"Do you sit here often?"

"Yes, I do."

"And what do you think about when you sit here?"

No one except Abba has ever asked me what I think. Maybe people like Abba and the pharaoh ask you what you think because they really want to know. So I tell him, "That I hope I never have to live in Goshen again." I feel his eyes on me, but I do not look up. I do not want to see what he might be thinking.

"You like it here?"

"I love it here!"

"And why is that?"

"Because everything is perfect," I tell him.

"But isn't everything perfect in Goshen?"

I am silent as I think about his question. Finally I say, "I don't know. I never thought about anything being perfect until the princess brought me here."

"But don't you believe in a god who is greater than Pharaoh? Doesn't this Ya make life perfect for you?" His voice is sharp, almost angry.

"I don't know much about Ya," I reply simply, which is true, and I don't want to talk about any of that. I want to know about the pharaoh.

He frowns. "Is something wrong?" he asks.

"No. Why do you ask?"

"You are staring at me as if my nose is on crooked or something."

I blush. "I am sorry. Please accept my apology. I was wondering about the snake on your headdress."

He chuckles and looks at Kakemour's father, who returns a weak smile. I don't know what is so funny. He turns back to me and explains. "That is the goddess Wadjet.

She protects Khemet. She also protected the goddess Eset and her newborn son, Hor, from the evil god Sutekh."

"Eset is beautiful!" I exclaim.

"Oh? And what do you know about Eset?"

"Nothing, except the princess has a beautiful mirror."

"Ah yes!" Then he is quiet. "That was Nefertari's mirror. I gave it to her some years ago and she gave it to Meryetamun."

"I did not know," I say apologetically.

"Did not know what?"

"That it was a gift from Queen Nefertari. I would not have used it had I known."

"You did no harm. What was it like to use it, Almah?"

"Oh, I have never held anything so beautiful in my life! I liked how heavy it felt in my hand and how it seemed to shine as if something were glowing inside. I liked how beautiful the goddess was, how proud and how strong she was even though she did not have on any clothes. And I liked seeing what I look like. I had only seen my face in the river, but looking at myself in the mirror—" I stop, embarrassed by what I was about to say.

"Go on."

I shake my head. "No. That's all right."

"I take it that you liked seeing yourself," the pharaoh says, as if he understands.

I nod. "Yes. Yes, I did. I had never known what I really look like."

"And what did you think?"

I am blushing. "That maybe I am pretty." I look up at

the pharaoh, hoping to see that sad smile. Instead tears are coming down his face.

"What's the matter?" I ask. "Did I say something wrong?"

He does not say anything for a long time. Finally he says, "You remind me so much of her. She was your age when I married her. I sit here with you, and you are so honest and open and inquisitive and full of life, and yes, beautiful. It is as if her *ka*—her spirit—is alive in you."

"I . . . I don't understand."

"You have the same heart as the queen," Kakemour puts in. "I noticed it when we spoke here a few days ago. The queen was not afraid, just as you are not."

That is what Ima said to Abba about me. "She is not afraid." Ima didn't like that. The pharaoh does.

Kakemour continues. "The other day when I saw you sitting here on the bench, it reminded me of all the times I saw the queen sitting here, and you looked just like her in how you seemed to want to take everything into your-self—the sun, the water, the birds, the air. I told my father and he told the pharaoh and the pharaoh wanted to see you for himself."

The pharaoh touches my arm lightly and then gets up and walks back toward the big palace. Queen Asetnefret has come out of the Women's Palace and moves toward him as if to speak, but he does not look in her direction. It is as if she does not exist to him.

"You made the pharaoh smile and laugh for the first time since the queen died," Kakemour whispers in my ear before he hurries to follow his father and the pharaoh. Only after they disappear from my view do I realize that everyone is staring at me, especially Asetnefret.

The next morning, I am eating breakfast when the princess comes to my room. "Someone is here to see you." Her voice sounds strained, and there is a look of both surprise and unhappiness on her face.

I go into the main room, where Ima and the princess are, and I am surprised to see Kakemour. Behind him are four servants. Two hold oblong golden boxes. The other two hold large baskets.

"Welcome in peace!" I greet him.

"In peace. In peace," he returns, smiling. "The pharaoh would be honored if you would accept these gifts."

I do not understand. A servant steps forward and, bowing, opens the box and places it at my feet. It is filled with bracelets, anklets, rings, earrings, and necklaces made of gold and jewels of reds and greens and blues. I cannot help but gasp at their beauty. But almost immediately another servant places her box beside the first one and opens it. More jewelry! I have never seen so many jewels in one place. The next servant places a basket on the floor and opens it. Inside are folded dresses of the purest white linen. The last servant opens her basket and reveals jars of ointments and colors and a mirror almost identical to the one the princess has. However, this one is more beautiful. The goddess has diamonds for eyes and a ruby for lips, and her golden feathers are embedded with jewels. As I hold it up, I hear a gasp from the princess.

I do not know what to say or do. I cannot believe all this is for me! Ima will never let me keep any of it. But then Kakemour says, "The pharaoh would also be honored if you would accept these two as your personal servants." He points to the ones who had carried the golden boxes. "Finally, the pharaoh would like you to have your own suite, a small suite, which is part of what was Queen Nefertari's large suite. The pharaoh would be honored to know that someone is living in part of the space that was hers."

I feel as if I am going to faint. My own suite! My own servants! The pharaoh wants me to live here for . . . for . . . forever, it seems. I will never have to go back to Goshen. I know I should say something, should express my thanks, but I could never put all I am feeling into words. Still, I must try.

"Please tell the son of Amon-Re, the Lord of the Two Lands, he whose prayers cause the sun to rise, that I am unworthy of such attention. I accept these gifts as expressions of his great generosity and hope that one day I will merit them."

Kakemour is impressed and so am I. "I will have your gifts taken to your rooms. You may occupy them anytime you are ready."

Kakemour and the four servants are scarcely out the door before Ima screams at me, "What did you do? No man gives a woman all that for nothing!"

"Ima!" I exclaim. "I have done nothing."

"Not yet! No man gives a woman gold and jewels without wanting something in return!"

I know what she is thinking. I know what she wants to call me, and I dare her to say it! I dare her!

"Tell her my father is not like that," the princess interjects. Although Ima and I spoke in Habiru, she understood Ima's tone of voice and angry eyes. "He is very generous to those who touch his heart."

I am surprised to hear the princess's voice break with bewilderment, hurt, and anger as she asks, "What did you do? I didn't know you knew my father. When did this happen?"

I tell her about yesterday, and as I translate for Ima, the princess starts crying softly. When I am done, the princess says wistfully, "When I was little I would sit on my mother's lap while the servants put on her makeup. She had two mirrors. She would never let me touch the one with the jewels in it, but she said that one day it would be mine. Maybe Father didn't know. Maybe he didn't care. I am not sure. But the mirror he gave to you is the one my mother said she was going to give to me."

"You can have it," I say immediately, meaning it. "I didn't know. I would feel better if you had it. I'm sure he didn't know your mother promised it to you."

The princess shakes her head. "I didn't see it before now. How could I have not? Probably because of your hair. But if I imagine you wearing a wig, it is obvious. You look like my mother did when I was a girl." She shakes her head again. "And I brought you here!" She stops. "I'm sorry, Almah. None of this is your fault. You are just being yourself. Who can fault you for that? And I can't blame Father, either. Thank you for offering me the mirror, but it is not that simple. You cannot refuse a gift from the pharaoh. Especially that gift. Don't you understand what his giving you my mother's mirror means?" she asks, hurt and anger coming back into her voice.

I don't know what she is talking about. I translate for Ima, and when I finish there is a long silence. Finally Ima looks at me and says, her voice filled with contempt, "You are now Pharaoh's daughter!"

now what to say. No. That is not true. There
ngs I could say but something stops me from
im about the ones he calls my "three moth-
he knows and is a little angry. That is why he
e.
ould any man need *three* of them?" he contin-
ig quietly. "Please understand. I love my moth-
s enough!"
at evening, when I am alone again in my
wonder why three women have raised me,
n who are so different and yet agree about
r me.
I am special to Ya. I wish I knew why, and
nts me to do. Mother tells me to be patient.
d of waiting and tired of not knowing what I
for. And how do I even know if I am waiting
? This could be how things are meant to be.
be the Habiru who is not really Habiru, the
who is not really Khemetian, the grandson of
who is not really his grandson. I will always
ig to be something I'm not and never know-
ally am.
ays I have trouble talking because I don't
hich "me" should be using my voice. She is
it. In my dreams I speak Habiru and Kheme-
nes both in the same sentence. But there's an-
, one I have not told anyone, not even her. I
say what I really feel because I am not always
feelings are mine or someone else's. I can feel

Part Two

Chap

OSIS, YO[U]
has thre[e]
It is [on the]
other side of the river.
me to drive a chariot.
desert. Looking back a[t]
the first time I held the
through the gates, and
the earth moves like wa[ter]

That seems so long
then. Now I am old en[ough inter-]
ested in women. Kake[r]
homes of noblemen w
marry the pharaoh's gr[a]
streets off the Avenue [of]
Village. If we keep wal[king]
in one of those places, [want]
me and I do, too. I hav[e]
enough to have an oc[casion]
want to do. I do not un[derstand]

I don't
are some t[hings]
talking to
ers." I thin[k]
is teasing [me]

"Why [contin-]
ues, chuckl[ing]
er, but one

Later t[hat]
suite, I, to[o]
three wom[en]
their love [for]

Ima say[s]
what he w
But I am ti[red]
am waiting
for anythin[g]
I will alway[s]
Khemetian
the pharao[h]
be pretend
ing who I [am]

Almah
know yet [who]
partially ri[ght]
tian, somet[hing]
other reas[on]
am afraid t[o]
sure if thos[e]

Part Two

Chapter One

MOSIS, YOU'RE THE ONLY man I know who has three mothers," Kakemour teases me. It is evening and we are walking on the other side of the river. This is where Kakemour taught me to drive a chariot. The earth is sandy here like the desert. Looking back across the river, I can still see myself the first time I held the reins as we came out of the stable, through the gates, and over the dike to this place where the earth moves like water.

That seems so long ago. I had nothing to worry about then. Now I am old enough to marry but I am not interested in women. Kakemour takes me to dinners at the homes of noblemen with beautiful daughters eager to marry the pharaoh's grandson, or to taverns on the side streets off the Avenue of the Crocodiles in the Workers' Village. If we keep walking in this direction we'll end up in one of those places, or worse. Kakemour worries about me and I do, too. I have no interest in women. I am old enough to have an occupation, but there is nothing I want to do. I do not understand what is wrong with me.

I don't know what to say. No. That is not true. There are some things I could say but something stops me from talking to him about the ones he calls my "three mothers." I think he knows and is a little angry. That is why he is teasing me.

"Why would any man need *three* of them?" he continues, chuckling quietly. "Please understand. I love my mother, but one is enough!"

Later that evening, when I am alone again in my suite, I, too, wonder why three women have raised me, three women who are so different and yet agree about their love for me.

Ima says I am special to Ya. I wish I knew why, and what he wants me to do. Mother tells me to be patient. But I am tired of waiting and tired of not knowing what I am waiting for. And how do I even know if I am waiting for anything? This could be how things are meant to be. I will always be the Habiru who is not really Habiru, the Khemetian who is not really Khemetian, the grandson of the pharaoh who is not really his grandson. I will always be pretending to be something I'm not and never knowing who I really am.

Almah says I have trouble talking because I don't know yet which "me" should be using my voice. She is partially right. In my dreams I speak Habiru and Khemetian, sometimes both in the same sentence. But there's another reason, one I have not told anyone, not even her. I am afraid to say what I really feel because I am not always sure if those feelings are mine or someone else's. I can feel